Enid Blyton

Mr Pink-Whistle Has Some Fun

Text illustrations by Stephen Dell
Cover illustration by Val Biro

D1100038

AWARD PUBLICATIONS LIMITED

Enid Blyton's Happy Days!

Snowball the Pony

Bimbo and Topsy

Run-About's Holiday

The Adventures of
Binkle and Flip

Binkle and Flip Misbehave

Mister Meddle's Mischief

Mister Meddle's Muddles

Merry
Mister Meddle

You're a Nuisance
Mister Meddle

Collect all the titles in the series!

The Adventures of
Mr Pink-Whistle

Mr Pink-Whistle
Has Some Fun

Mr Pink-Whistle's
Party

Mr Pink-Whistle
Interferes

Hello
Mr Twiddle!

Mr Twiddle
in Trouble Again

Don't Be Silly,
Mr Twiddle!

Mr Twiddle
in Trouble Again

Shuffle
the Shoemaker

For further information on Enid Blyton please visit *www.blyton.com*

ISBN 978-1-84135-654-9

Illustrations copyright © Award Publications Limited

First published 1950 & 1955 by George Newnes

First published by Award Publications Limited 2004
This edition first published 2010

Published by Award Publications Limited,
The Old Riding School, The Welbeck Estate,
Worksop, Nottinghamshire, S80 3LR

11 2

Printed in the United Kingdom

Contents

Chapter 1

Mr Pink-Whistle Has Some Fun

One day Mr Pink-Whistle was sitting reading by the fire, when he heard a knock at his front door. It was rather a timid little knock – rat-a-tat-tat.

'Sooty,' said Pink-Whistle to his big black cat, 'see who's at the door, please.'

Sooty scurried to the door and opened it. Outside stood two little girls, looking rather scared. 'Oh,' said one, when she saw Sooty, 'this must be Mr Pink-Whistle's house, because we know he has a cat called Sooty who looks after him! Please, are you Sooty?'

'That's my name,' said Sooty. 'Do come in.'

The two little girls went in and wiped their feet very carefully on the mat. Sooty took them into the room where Mr Pink-Whistle sat. He smiled at them.

'Oh, you're just exactly like Mr Pink-Whistle in our stories!' said one little girl. 'You are, really!'

'I'm glad,' said Pink-Whistle. 'As a matter of fact I always do look like myself, of course. What are your names?'

'I'm Katie and she's Jessie,' said Katie. 'And we've come to ask your help. We've heard so many stories about you, and how you go round the world putting wrong things right – so we thought we'd ask you to put something right for us. Will you, please, Mr Pink-Whistle?'

'Of course,' said Pink-Whistle. 'Sooty, bring some biscuits and lemonade.'

So, over biscuits and lemonade, the two little girls told kind Mr Pink-Whistle their troubles, just as you would if you had something to tell him.

'You see, it's like this,' said Katie, 'there are two boys in our village who are very cruel and unkind, Mr Pink-Whistle. They throw stones at the cats and dogs, they take birds' eggs out of the nests, they hide round corners and jump out at us, and –'

8

'Yes, and they knock at doors and run away, and they go to the greengrocer's and take apples and oranges when he's not looking,' said Jessie. 'And, oh dear, lately they have been lying in wait for Katie and me and the other girls, and taking our dolls from us.'

'And they broke my doll,' said Katie, with tears in her eyes. 'They dropped her on the pavement. So we've come to you to ask if you could put things right for us. We are all getting so afraid of Tom and Len.'

'I hope you don't think we're telling tales,' said Jessie. 'We just simply didn't know what to do. And now the two boys are frightening

9

babies in their prams by booing at them when they pass. The worst of it is that their parents think they are wonderful boys and won't believe a word against them. So what are we to do?'

Mr Pink-Whistle looked very solemn. He handed round the biscuits for the third time. 'This is very serious,' he said. 'Serious for you because you are frightened – and serious for the boys because they will grow up into just the kind of people we don't want. Hmmmmmm! I must certainly think of something.'

'We knew you would,' said Katie. 'What will you do?'

'I don't quite know,' said Pink-Whistle. 'I'll think about it. I'd like it to be something that will teach the parents to be sensible about their boys too. You know, as a rule, if children grow up bad it's the fault of the fathers and mothers.'

'Yes, we've noticed that,' said Katie. 'If you've got nice parents, you're usually nice yourself.

The clock struck four. Katie got up at once. 'We must go,' she said, 'or we shall be late for tea. Mother will worry about us. Thank you,

10

Mr Pink-Whistle, for listening to us, and for the lemonade and biscuits.'

'Yes, thank you very much,' said Jessie.

'What very nice parents you both must have!' said Pink-Whistle, shaking hands with them. 'Now you needn't go red! You've just told me that nice parents have nice children and, as I can see you are both nice, I know what your parents are like!'

The two little girls went away, excited and pleased. They trusted Mr Pink-Whistle. He would do something to stop those two boys and put things right.

He did! He thought and he thought, and then the next day he called Sooty. 'I'm going off to that village the girls came from,' he said. 'I'm going to make myself invisible so that no one can see me. And I'm going to find those boys – and their parents too – and give them a shock. I'll be back when my job is finished, Sooty.'

'Very good, Master,' said Sooty. 'Just let me brush your hat for you. What a pity there aren't more people like you in the world, always trying to put bad things right!'

Pink-Whistle went off. Sooty couldn't see him when he got to the gate, because he had already made himself quite invisible. Ah, Pink-Whistle could see a lot of peculiar things going on when he was invisible – nobody knew he was there then!

He soon found the two boys. He saw them hiding behind a wall, waiting for an old woman to come. They had water-pistols in their hands. Just as the old woman came round the wall the boys squirted their pistols.

The water went right into the old woman's face. She gasped, and dropped her basket. The eggs in it broke, and the yellow yolk dripped out on to the pavement.

'Oh! Oh! What is it? I've been shot! Oh, what has happened to me?' groaned the old

woman, sitting down on the kerb with her head in her hands.

Pink-Whistle saw someone coming to help her. He quickly followed the two boys, who had run away at once, laughing. They got on a bus. Pink-Whistle got on too. Nobody saw him, of course, nobody at all. He sat down just behind the two boys.

He waited till the bus had started, then he spoke in a loud and angry voice.

'Which boys on this bus frightened an old lady just now? Who shot her with a water-pistol and made her drop her basket and break her eggs?'

There was a startled silence in the bus. All the passengers looked round to see who was speaking. The boys went red from their foreheads down to their necks, and hardly dared to breathe. Who knew all this? Was it a policeman?

'I can see those boys,' said Pink-Whistle, in a loud and stern voice. 'I CAN SEE THEM!'

In fright the two boys leapt off the bus. Pink-Whistle went too, though they didn't see him. 'Now we've got to walk home,' said one boy, crossly. 'Who was that shouting at us in the bus?'

13

'Pooh! What does it matter?' said the other boy. 'Come on, Len – let's ring a few bells and run away!'

Pink-Whistle followed Len and Tom. They crept up to a front door and pressed the bell. Then they ran away. They went to another door and did the same thing. Pink-Whistle frowned. He walked behind them down the street.

When the boys came into the high street Pink-Whistle began to shout loudly again. 'Where are those two boys who rang the bell and ran away? Where are they? Bring them here to be punished!'

Everyone was startled to hear this sudden voice coming from nowhere. As for the two boys they were terrified! They looked all round, and people began to point at them. 'They must be the two boys, look! Somebody must be after them!'

The boys fled at once. Pink-Whistle followed them, still invisible. Round the corner they met a small girl with a little puppy. Len pounced on the dog and the little girl screamed.

'Don't! Don't hurt him! He's only little!'

Tom took up an old tin lying in a nearby

ditch and began to tie it to the tail of the
frightened puppy. The little pup bit at him
and squealed. Len scolded it.

Pink-Whistle's voice boomed out again.

'Where are those boys? Where are those
two bad boys?'

Len and Tom clutched at each other in
fright. That voice again! Who was following
them? They left the little girl and the scared
puppy and ran at top speed down the road.

The little girl felt something pressed into
her hand. 'Go and buy yourself some sweets,'
said a kind voice in her ear – but there was
nobody there – how very, very strange!

Pink-Whistle followed the boys. They both
turned in at the same gate. 'My mother and
father are in with yours this afternoon,' said
Len. 'We're all going to the pictures together
tonight. So I can come in with you.'

'Aha! Good!' thought Pink-Whistle, and he
went in at the gate, too, round the back and
in at the kitchen door with the two boys. They
didn't see him, of course.

The boys slammed the door and clattered
in without wiping their feet. Len went to the
larder door and grinned at Tom. They both
stuck their dirty fingers into a jar of jam and

licked them. Then they took some plums out of a pie and ate those.

'Not a word!' said Tom and winked at Len. Then they both went into the sitting-room. Their parents were there, talking.

'Well – have you been good boys today?' asked one of the mothers.

'Oh, yes,' said Tom. 'Both top of our class, and we came straight home as you said, and here we are.'

'Who went into the larder just now and helped themselves to jam and plums out of the pie?' said a loud voice suddenly. 'Where are the boys who did that mean thing? Stealing, I call it.'

There was a sudden silence. The parents looked at one another to see who had spoken. The boys went as red as beetroots.

'Who said that?' said a father, at last. 'How strange that voice sounded! I don't like it. Come on – let's go to the pictures. We all look scared! I'm sure the boys wouldn't take anything from the larder.'

'But they did! Didn't you, boys? said Pink-Whistle's stern voice. The boys stood trembling and didn't say a word.

One of the fathers got up, looking pale. 'Come along. We'll go. There's something strange going on here. Somebody calling through the window or down the chimney or something.'

They all went out. They caught a bus and so did Pink-Whistle. As soon as they were all seated on the bus, he began again.

'Where are the boys who scared that little girl and tied a can to her puppy's tail? Where are they? Bring them to me!'

Again Tom and Len went red and trembled. Everyone looked at them. A man spoke up from the corner. 'Who is it that

17

wants to know about those bad boys? There they are on that seat there, shaking in their shoes. Come and get them!'

The boys leapt off the bus in fright, and their parents followed, troubled and puzzled. They went into the cinema without a word – but each mother and father was thinking hard. Why was that voice following them? Why did their boys look so red and ashamed?

And dear me, the voice came into the cinema with them as well! Every time there was a quiet piece in the film the voice – speaking in a loud whisper this time.

'Who scared the old woman with a water-pistol? Who rang the bells and ran away? Who frightened the little girl with the dog? Who has got parents who don't know what their boys are up to? Who went into the larder and –'

Len began to cry. Tom went very white this time, instead of red. The parents felt so upset that they couldn't watch the film any more. One by one they rose and went out. Pink-Whistle followed them.

They went home to Len's house. Pink-Whistle slipped in with them, too. The parents faced the boys.

'What's all this about? Where does this voice come from? Is it true what it keeps saying?'

'No,' said Len.

'No,' said Tom, his head down.

'Who tells untruths to their parents?' began the voice again. 'Who lies in wait for little girls and breaks their dolls? Who throws stones at dogs and cats. WHO, WHO, WHO?'

'We do, we do!' sobbed Len and Tom, suddenly, almost scared out of their lives. 'We do all those things. We won't any more. We won't!'

'I'll see you don't!' said Len's father, angrily. 'To think you do these things behind our backs and pretend to be so good to our faces!'

'They want scolding,' said Tom's father. 'We've not been firm enough with them.'

'Oh, Tom, oh, Len – how could you do things like that?' wailed their mothers.

'Partly your fault, partly your fault!' said the voice again. 'Why don't you look after your children better? I'll look after them! I'll tell the world about them! I'll –'

'No, no, no!' cried Len. 'Go away, whoever you are. You frighten me. Go away!'

'I'm going,' said Pink-Whistle solemnly. 'I'm going. I'm going.' His voice got softer and softer. Then suddenly and most frighteningly it got loud again. 'But I'm coming back if you don't keep your word. Yes – I'm COMING back!'

He went then, back to his little cottage and to Sooty, feeling quite tired out. 'I think I've put that right,' he said to Sooty. 'But you never know!'

Good old Pink-Whistle. He certainly has put it right. Those boys – and their parents, too – are quite, quite different. Oh, dear – I

do hope I never hear his voice booming out
because I've done something wrong. I would
be so ashamed, wouldn't you?

Chapter 2

Mr Pink-Whistle
Goes to School

Mr Pink-Whistle was walking down the road wondering if the fishmonger had any kippers for himself and Sooty, his cat, when four girls and two boys came running along.

'Quick!' said one. 'Get round the corner before Harry and George see us!'

They shot round the corner – and then came the sound of pattering footsteps behind Mr Pink-Whistle once more, and along came two big boys, almost knocking him over.

Mr Pink-Whistle went spinning into the gutter and just saved himself from sitting down hard by clutching at a lamp-post.

The two boys didn't say they were sorry, they didn't even stop! They rushed round the corner after the smaller children.

'Good gracious!' said Mr Pink-Whistle, letting go the lamp-post. 'What unpleasant boys! Who are they, I wonder?'

He went round the corner. He saw Harry and George pouncing on the smaller children and taking their hats and caps away. They sent them sailing up into the trees and over the hedges!

'You are hateful,' said a small girl, beginning to cry. 'You're always playing horrid tricks, and making us take the blame!'

'You hid my French book yesterday and I got into trouble for it,' said Joan.

'You spilt my drink all over the floor, and I had to stay in,' said Peter. 'I know you did it! It's just the kind of thing you always do.'

'Yes – and then you leave us to bear the blame,' said Doris.' And if we tell tales of you you pinch our faces and tramp on our toes!'

Harry pounced on Doris and pulled her hair so hard that she squealed.

'Let go!' she said.

Mr Pink-Whistle made himself invisible. He

crept up to Harry, caught hold of his hair and tugged hard.

'Oh!' said Harry, and swung round. George was just near by. 'Did you pull my hair? What do you think you're doing?'

'I didn't touch you,' said George. 'Don't be silly!'

Then the two boys glared at one another and put up their fists to fight. The other children saw their chance and ran off at once. Let them fight! They wouldn't bother the others then!

Mr Pink-Whistle didn't like the two boys at all. He took a look at them. Their faces were hard. It wouldn't be any good talking to them, or pleading with them to be better. They would laugh.

'No – the only thing is to do the same things to them that they do to others,' decided Mr Pink-Whistle. 'I shall go to school with these children this afternoon. Ha – there'll be a bit of fun then! But not for George or Harry!'

He waited for the children that afternoon and then walked along beside them, unseen. He saw how they all ran away from George and Harry, and how frightened of the two big boys they were.

'A couple of bullies!' said Mr Pink-Whistle. 'Well, well – bullies are always cowards, so we'll just see what Harry and George do when unpleasant things begin to happen to them. They shall take the blame for things I do this afternoon, in return for making others take the blame for things that they so often have done.'

He went into the schoolroom with Harry and George and the rest of their class. He noticed where the two big boys sat and went over to them. Nobody could see him. He was quite invisible, of course.

When George was bending down to pick up a dropped pencil Mr Pink-Whistle opened his desk lid and let it drop with a terrific BANG!

Everyone jumped. The teacher frowned 'George! There's no need to make that noise.'

'I didn't,' said George, indignantly. 'I was bending down. Someone else must have banged my desk-lid.'

'Was it you, Harry?' asked the teacher. Harry always sat next to George.

'No, it wasn't,' said Harry, rudely.

Well, Mr Pink-Whistle managed to bang George's desk-lid twice more, and the teacher began to blame Harry, because George was so very indignant that she felt sure it couldn't be his fault.

The two boys glared at one another. Then Mr Pink-Whistle tipped a pile of books off Harry's desk when he wasn't looking!

'HARRY!' said the teacher.

'I didn't do it,' said Harry, angrily. 'Make George pick up my books. He must have done that.'

'I didn't,' said George. 'Yah!'

'Boys, boys!' said the teacher. 'George,

come up here and write on the board for me. Write down the homework notes for tomorrow.'

George went up sulkily. He took up the chalk and began to write on the board. Mr Pink-Whistle was just behind him, invisible.

He took George's hand and began to guide the piece of chalk. And do you know what he wrote? He wrote this:

'Harry is a silly donkey. Harry is a dunce. Harry is –'

George was horrified. Whatever was the chalk doing? It seemed to be writing by itself, and he couldn't stop it. And look what it was

writing too! Whatever would his teacher say? Where was the duster? He must rub out the rude writing at once!

Aha! Mr Pink-Whistle had taken the duster, of course. He had thrown it up to the top of a picture. George couldn't see it anywhere.

The children saw what George had written, and they began to nudge one another and giggle. The teacher turned to see what George was doing behind her – and dear me, she saw what he had written on the blackboard!

'GEORGE!' she said angrily. 'How dare you do that? What in the world are you thinking of? Rub it out at once.'

'I didn't mean to,' said poor George. 'It felt as if the chalk was writing by itself.'

'Oh, don't be so silly,' said the teacher. 'My goodness me – look where the duster has been thrown to! Did you throw it there, George? You'd better lose ten marks straight away for your silly behaviour this afternoon!'

Harry laughed like anything. He was angry with George for writing rude things about him on the board. Mr Pink-Whistle waited till George was back in his seat and then he pulled Harry's hair quite hard.

Harry jumped and glared round at George. Mr Pink-Whistle tugged at George's hair then. George jumped and glared round at Harry.

'Stop that!' they said to each other, and the teacher banged on her desk for quiet.

Well, Mr Pink-Whistle quite enjoyed himself that afternoon and so did all the class, except Harry and George. Harry's ruler shot off his desk. George's pencil-box upset all over the floor. Harry's shoe-laces came mysteriously undone three times. George's socks kept slipping down to his ankles, and his shirt buttons came undone at his neck. It was all very extraordinary.

They all went out to play for ten minutes. Mr Pink-Whistle went with them. He kicked Harry's ball into the next-door garden. He tripped George up twice and sent him rolling over and over. The two boys got very angry indeed, because they both felt certain it was the other one playing tricks.

After a few minutes Mr Pink-Whistle went indoors. He went to Harry's desk and put half his books into George's. He put George's pencils into Harry's box. That was the kind of thing the two boys were always doing to other

people. Well, let them see if they liked it or not!

They didn't like it a bit. Harry wailed aloud when he found half his books gone, because the teacher was always very cross when anyone was careless with books. And George was furious to find his best pencils missing.

'Who's taken them? Wait till I find out!' he cried angrily. 'Teacher – all my best pencils have gone!'

They were found in Harry's box almost at once, and George almost flew at him in rage. He would have hit him then and there if the teacher hadn't suddenly discovered that Harry's books were in George's desk! She was really disgusted.

'I thought you two boys were friends. Look at this – your books in George's desk, Harry, and all George's pencils in your box. You ought to be ashamed of yourselves. Any more nonsense from either of you and you will stay in for half an hour.'

Well, there was quite a lot of nonsense of course – but it was from Mr Pink-Whistle, not from the boys! He upset George's paint-pot all over his painting – a thing that George himself did to somebody almost every painting lesson! And he smudged Harry's best writing when he wasn't looking. And that, too, was something that Harry was very fond of doing to the smaller children.

The teacher was cross. 'Stay in for half an hour, both of you,' she said. 'I don't care if you are going out to a party. You can be half an hour late.'

'But you know it's my cousin's birthday party,' said George, indignantly. 'I can't be late.'

'I know all about the party – and I'm afraid you will be late, both of you!' said the teacher, firmly. The two boys glared at one another. Each felt sure it was the other who had got him into all this trouble!

They had to stay in for half an hour and do most of their work again. Then they said a sulky goodbye and went out.

As soon as they got out in the road they began to quarrel. 'I suppose you think you were very clever this afternoon!' said George, angrily. 'Well, take that!'

And he hit Harry hard on the back. Mr Pink-Whistle grinned. A fight? Well, he would join in as well. He would repay both George and Harry for the nasty treatment that they had many a time dealt out to the younger children.

So, quite invisible, he hopped in and out, dealing a pinch here and a tug there, and making the boys yell in pain, and go for each other all the more.

Biff! That was George hitting Harry on the nose. It began to bleed.

Smack! That was Harry hitting George on his right eye. It began to go black at once.

Thud! That was Mr Pink-Whistle doing his share!

BIFF-BANG! That was both boys at once – and they fell over, crash, into a muddy puddle. They sat up, howling.

'Let's stop,' wept George. 'My eye hurts.

And your nose is bleeding. We're terribly late for the party. We shall miss all the good things at tea.'

So, sniffing and snuffling, muddy, wet and very much the worse for wear, the two boys arrived at their cousin's house. But when their aunt saw them, she was very cross indeed.

'George! Harry! How can you come to a party looking like that? Have you been fighting one another? You should be ashamed of yourselves. One with a black eye and one with a bleeding nose! And so dirty and untidy too. I won't let you in. You shan't come to the party!'

And she slammed the door in their faces. They went howling down the street, very sorry for themselves.

Mr Pink-Whistle began to think they might have learnt their lesson. He suddenly appeared beside them, a kind little man with pointed ears.

'Come and have tea with me,' he said. 'I live not far off with my cat Sooty.'

So they went with him, still sniffing. He made them wash and brush their hair. He stopped Harry's nose from bleeding, and he bathed George's eye. Then he sat them down to bread and butter and honey and a seed-cake.

'You're very kind,' said George, surprised.

'I'm not always,' said Mr Pink-Whistle, solemnly. 'Sometimes, when I see mean, unkind people I get that way myself – just to punish them, you know. I've had a good time this afternoon, punishing two nasty little boys. My word, they were horrid little things – always teasing the smaller ones and getting them into trouble.'

The two boys gazed at him, afraid.

'You've no idea of the things I did!' said Mr Pink-Whistle, passing them the seed-cake.

'My, the tricks I played in their class this afternoon – and what a time I had when those boys fought. I fought, too – biff, thud!'

The boys looked at one another uncomfortably. They both felt very scared.

'You know, I always think that if mean, unkind people get treated meanly and unkindly themselves sometimes, they learn how horrid it is,' said Mr Pink-Whistle. 'Of course – they sometimes need more than one lesson – perhaps two, or four, or even six!'

He looked hard at the two boys. They looked back. 'Sir,' said George, in a small voice. 'We shan't need more than that one lesson. I promise you that.'

'I promise you, too,' said Harry, in a whisper. 'It's – it's very kind of you, sir, to take us home and give us this tea – when you know we're mean.'

'Bless us all, you can come again as often as you like – so long as you don't need another lesson from me, but only a nice tea!' said kind Mr Pink-Whistle. 'Now do take another piece of cake each – just to show there's no ill-feeling between us!'

Well, they did, of course. And, so far as I know, Mr Pink-Whistle hasn't had to give them another lesson – yet! But he would, you know, if they broke their promise. He's kind – but he's fierce, too, when he's putting wrong things right!

Chapter 3

Mr Pink-Whistle Laughs!

Mr Pink-Whistle had been to see an old friend of his, and had just said goodbye.

'I must catch the bus!' he said. 'I shall be late for dinner if I don't, and Sooty, my cat, won't be very pleased!'

But just as he reached the corner where the bus-stop was, he saw the bus rumbling away down the road. He had missed it!

'Never mind – I'll buy some sandwiches and go and eat them in this park,' he thought, and off he went to get some tomato and sardine sandwiches. Then he made his way to the park, and sat down on a seat.

It was sunny and warm, and Mr Pink-Whistle felt happy. He sat there eating his sandwiches, throwing crumbs to the sparrows and chaffinches around. And then he felt sleepy.

He closed his eyes and nodded a little. Soon he was dreaming – and in his dream he heard someone crying.

'Don't! Don't!' he heard, and woke up with a jump. A little girl was coming down the path, with tears running down her cheeks. Mr Pink-Whistle sat up straight at once. Was there something here that he could put right?

'Hello, hello!' said Pink-Whistle, as the little girl came by. 'What's wrong?'

'He's taken my biscuits,' said the little girl. 'And he's eaten them!'

'Dear me – who has?' said Pink-Whistle, wishing that he hadn't eaten all his sandwiches, so that he could offer the little girl some.

'That boy – the boy who rushes out at us,' said the little girl, crying again. 'I don't know his name. He hides in the bushes while we're playing – and then he rushes out and takes our things. There's another boy, too, this morning. They took Fred's ball, and Nora's balloon.'

'Look, here's fifty pence to buy some more biscuits,' said Pink-Whistle. 'Don't cry any more. I'll see to these boys.'

'Oh, thank you!' said the small girl, and she scrubbed her wet cheeks with her hanky. 'They're up there, look – by the children's playground. But you'd better be careful. They might knock off your hat and run away with it!'

'Good gracious me!' said Pink-Whistle, astonished. He thought he would go over to the children's playground and watch for these two boys.

'I'll make myself invisible,' he thought. 'Then there won't be any chance of my hat being knocked off. So that's the kind of boys they are, is it? Aha – they certainly want someone to deal with them!'

He muttered a few magic words under his breath, and hey presto, he was gone! Not a bit of him was to be seen; he was quite invisible. He set off up the path towards the children's playground, listening to the calls and shouts that came from there. It sounded as if quite a lot of children were playing games.

He came to a seat just by the playground and sat down. There were swings and see-saws there, there were children playing with bats and balls, there was even a pond where some were sailing little boats.

Pink-Whistle watched. He couldn't see any bad boys at all. Everyone seemed to be playing happily. Then he saw a boy coming up the path to go to the pond, carrying a fine little ship with a sail.

Pink-Whistle was watching him when there came a rustle in the bushes just behind him, and out leapt a big boy, making Pink-Whistle jump almost out of his skin.

He pushed the small boy over, snatched his

ship, and leapt back into the bushes. There was the sound of giggling and whispering, and Pink-Whistle guessed the second boy was there too.

The other boy sat up, dazed, for he had knocked his head hard on the path. 'Where's my ship?' he shouted. 'Give it back to me!'

But nobody came to give it back, and he went mournfully to the playground, looking everywhere for someone with his ship. Then out came the two boys from the bushes, nudging one another and giggling. One of them had the ship. They walked boldly over to the pond and set the boat on the water.

The boy who owned the ship came up at once. 'That's mine!' he said. 'You snatched it from me just now. You give it back.'

'Ooh, you fibber! It's ours,' said the two boys together. 'You just try and get it from us. We'll knock you over!'

Other children came round. 'I bet you took his ship!' cried a small girl with a pram. 'You took my brother's cap the other day. I saw you!'

One of the big boys reached over to the pram, took out the doll that sat there and threw it into the water – splash! The little girl

41

screamed. But nobody dared to do anything
to the two big boys. Another boy waded into
the water and brought back the doll for the
little girl – but just as he handed it to her, the
second big boy snatched it and once again
the poor doll was thrown into the water.

And then, to Pink-Whistle's delight, up
came the park-keeper! 'Now, now!' he said.
'What's all this? Are you making nuisances of
yourselves again, you boys? Clear off at once!'

The two boys laughed at him. One gave
him a push that almost sent him into the
pond, and the other knocked off his peaked
cap. All the children watched in silence.

'Now then! You stop that! I'll report you!' shouted the park-keeper angrily. 'Get my cap!'

'Get it yourself!' said one of the boys. 'Report us! Why, you don't even know our names!'

The park-keeper ran at him, but the boy dodged and took to his heels, followed by his friend. They could run fast and they disappeared round the bushes at top speed.

'They've not gone home,' said another boy. 'I bet they're waiting till the park-keeper's gone, then they'll be here again. I wish a policeman would come.'

The park-keeper went off, fuming with rage, and the children began to play again. Pink-Whistle kept a careful watch – were those bad boys anywhere near? He hoped so. He was going to have a bit of fun with them!

Yes – they were there – in those bushes. Ah – here they come, giggling and pushing one another. They ran at a boy with a cricket bat and pulled it out of his hand. They took a ball from someone else and began to have a game. If anyone came near they swiped at him with the bat.

Pink-Whistle got up. He was still invisible,

and he walked among the children unseen. He went up to the big boy with the bat and twisted it out of his hand. The boy stared in amazement. 'Here – who took my bat. Hey – what's happening?'

Pink-Whistle was holding the bat – but as he was invisible, it looked just as if the bat were hanging by itself in the air! Pink-Whistle raised it and gave the boy a tap on the behind with it. The boy yelled.

Then Pink-Whistle snatched off the boy's cap, and ran away with it. It looked strange to see a cap bobbing along by itself in the air! Pink-Whistle put it on the head of the little statue on the water-fountain. How strange it was to see a cap put itself there! Nobody could see Pink-Whistle, of course.

The little man went back to the two surprised boys. He undid the tie belonging to the second boy – and dear me, away went the tie through the air, too, blowing in the wind as Pink-Whistle carried it in his hand! He tied it high up in a bush.

'Here! What's happening?' cried the two boys, beginning to be scared. 'Let's take the ship and go home!'

But now the invisible Pink-Whistle was back

again, and took the ship himself, right out of the hand of one of the big boys! He walked over to the boy who owned it, and put it into his hand. It looked exactly as if the boat had flown by itself through the air to its owner!

The two boys began to run – but Pink-Whistle ran too. He caught each of them by their belts, and down they went. They were bruised, and one burst into sobs. As the boy sat there Pink-Whistle undid his shoes and

slid them off – and to everyone's amazement, the shoes appeared to trot through the air all by themselves! 'My shoes!' yelled the boy. 'Look, my shoes!'

Somebody snatched at the shoes as they travelled through the air, held by the invisible Mr Pink-Whistle, and threw them into the pond – splash – splash – splash! They sank at once.

'Oh, good! That's what those boys did to my doll!' cried the girl with the pram. Everyone began to laugh. They pointed at the two boys, who had now got up from the ground. 'It serves you right, it serves you right!' they cried.

One of the big boys lost his temper, and rushed at a boy playing with a ball. He kicked it right out of his hands, and it rose in the air, and went into a tree. It stayed there, caught in a branch.

'That's my new ball!' yelled the little boy.

'He'll get it for you!' cried a voice that seemed to come from nowhere. 'Go on, you big bully, climb the tree and get the ball!' And the invisible Mr Pink-Whistle ran the big boy to the tree, caught hold of him by his shorts and jerked him up. He pushed him and prodded him, and the boy, yelling with fright, found himself forced to climb up and get the ball.

It bounced down, the big boy began to climb down himself – but dear me, what was this? A circle of angry children closed round the bottom of the tree, and a boy with a bat raised it high.

'What a chance to give him back some of the biffs he gave us!' he cried. 'Come on, bully – climb down – see what will happen to you then!'

The big boy yelled to his friend. 'Come and help me, come on!' But his friend was no longer there! He had run off at top speed, scared at all these peculiar happenings.

The first boy climbed back into the tree again, and sat up there, shivering with fright, looking down at the children. Was all this a horrid dream?

A little whisper went round, 'I say – can it be Mr Pink-Whistle doing all this? You know – it might be!'

Ooooh! Mr Pink-Whistle. The children stared at one another and then looked all round. But they couldn't see him, of course. 'Please, please, if you're here, let us see you!'

47

cried the little girl with the pram. 'We know all about you!'

Pink-Whistle was pleased. Now, how did they know all about him? He muttered the magic words that made him become visible again – and the watching children saw a shadow first of all, and then a shape – and then Mr Pink-Whistle himself smiling all over his face! They crowded round him in joy.

'You always put things right, don't you! Oh, Mr Pink-Whistle, we never thought you'd be here this morning! You did give those boys a fright!'

Mr Pink-Whistle saw an ice-cream man

coming along, riding down the path with his little cart. He called him. 'Ice-creams for everyone, please,' he said.

The boy up the tree sat listening in amazement. Yes – he had heard about Mr Pink-Whistle, too. Goodness – to think he had been behaving so badly when the little man came by! He felt ashamed and afraid. He began to slide gently down the tree, hoping to creep away unseen and go home. But he suddenly saw something at the bottom of the tree, and stopped.

It was a dog! Had Mr Pink-Whistle put it there to wait for him and bite him? The boy clambered back again at top speed, and looked longingly at the big ice-creams.

Pink-Whistle hadn't put the dog there, of course. One of the small boys had placed his toy dog there while he went to eat his ice-cream – and will you believe it, he forgot all about it, and left it there, at the foot of the tree. Soon all the children went with Mr Pink-Whistle to the bus-stop, and the scared boy up the tree was left alone, guarded by a toy dog! And there he stayed till the park-keeper came along and found him.

'Goodbye,' said Pink-Whistle, to the

delighted children, as he climbed into the bus. 'Don't worry about those boys any more. Just say "Now where's Mr Pink-Whistle?" if you have any trouble – and they'll run like the wind! Goodbye!'

Chapter 4

Mr Pink-Whistle Has a Peep

Every day when Mr Pink-Whistle had to go down to the village to do a bit of shopping, he passed a small house.

One evening when he passed it, the curtains were not drawn, but there was a light inside, so that Mr Pink-Whistle couldn't help seeing into the room.

It was a playroom. He could see that because the wall paper was a nursery rhyme one, there was a big rocking-horse in a corner, and a doll's house on the floor. A teddy bear sat on a cupboard and a doll's cot stood by the wall.

How Pink-Whistle loved playrooms. He thought toy trains and rocking-horses and toy farms and bricks were lovely. So he had a very good look inside.

And after that, every time he passed the playroom he took a peep. He knew the children wouldn't mind, because all children love old Pink-Whistle.

Two little girls lived in the playroom. Mr Pink-Whistle thought they must be twins, and he was right. One was Rose and the other was Daisy. They played together every single day when they came back from school.

When Mr Pink-Whistle peeped in at the window the girls were always playing the same game. They were playing with their dolls.

They had a very large family of dolls. If you asked them the names of their family they could tell you straight off.

'Angela, Josephine, Rosemary, Jennifer and, of course, Baby the baby doll. It's too young to have a name.'

Mr Pink-Whistle loved to see Rose and Daisy with their dolls. They dressed and undressed them, they bathed them, they powdered them, they even filled a bottle with what looked like milk and tried to feed the baby doll with it.

'How they love their dolls!' thought Mr Pink-Whistle. 'I wonder if their mother has a baby – these two children could almost look after it for her!'

But she hadn't. She only had Rose and Daisy, and they were nine years old. They each had a pram for their dolls and took them out for walks. They washed their dolls' clothes, and Mummy, even let them iron them. Really, Pink-Whistle got a great deal of fun in peeping at Rose and Daisy and seeing all they did.

Then one day he passed another small house on his way back home. Usually the curtains were drawn and he didn't know what was inside the windows of the room he passed. But this evening the curtains were not drawn and a light was shining there.

Mr Pink-Whistle peeped in, hoping to see some more children. All he saw was a baby crying in a cot, and dear me – what was that on the floor?

Mr Pink-Whistle tried to see, and then he gave a cry and ran round the house to the front door. He knocked and knocked. No answer. He ran to the back door and that was open.

In he went and made his way to the room he had peeped into. On the floor lay a young woman, groaning. Mr Pink-Whistle lifted her up gently.

'What's the matter?' he asked.

'Oh, I feel so ill,' said the young woman. 'My husband is away and I tried to lift something too heavy for me. I've hurt my back.'

'I'll get you to hospital,' said Mr Pink-Whistle.

'No, no!' cried the young woman. 'There's a baby. I can't part from him. I can't. All I want is a nice rest tonight and I'll be all right in the morning. I was just going to bath my baby and feed him when I fainted.'

'Shall I get a neighbour in to help you?' said kind Mr Pink-Whistle.

'No. They don't know anything about young babies,' said the young woman.

'Oh, dear – what shall I do? I just want help tonight, that's all.'

'Well – I could bath a baby and feed it myself,' said Mr Pink-Whistle, 'but I've got a better idea than that. Wait here and I'll fetch someone at once.'

He went out of the front door and ran to the house where Rose and Daisy lived. He knocked on the window of their playroom.

The twins came at once, in great surprise. They stared at the funny little man at the window.

'You won't know who I am,' began Mr Pink-Whistle, 'but –'

'We do know who you are,' said Rose, suddenly, staring hard. 'You're Mr Pink-Whistle. You are, you are! We've got a book about you, so we know you well.'

'How strange,' said Mr Pink-Whistle. 'You're quite right. That's who I am. Well, my dears, I want a bit of help and I've come to you for it.'

'Oh – Mr Pink-Whistle! Do you really want us to help you!' said both twins at once. 'We'd simply love to.'

'It's like this,' said Pink-Whistle. 'I've been peeping in at you for some time now, and I can see how kind and loving you are to your dolls – especially to your baby doll – and now I want a bit of help with a real live baby, whose mother is ill. I suppose you couldn't come and bath it and feed it this evening?'

The twins' eyes nearly fell out of their heads. 'A live baby,' said Rose. 'How wonderful!'

'We've always wished our dolls were alive,' said Daisy. 'Where's this baby? We'll just have to tell our mother we're going out for a bit.'

'Well, tell her, and come along,' said Mr Pink-Whistle, feeling almost as excited as the twins. They ran to tell their mother and then they went off with Mr Pink-Whistle.

'We simply love our dolls, but we'd love a real baby a hundred times more,' said Rose. 'But not even our aunts have got a baby. So we have to make do with dolls.'

'Here we are,' said Mr Pink-Whistle and led them in at a little front door. The young woman was on the bed, still looking pale. She looked surprised when she saw the twins.

'Oh, I know these little girls,' she said. 'I often meet them out, wheeling their dolls' prams. But they wouldn't know how to bath and feed my precious baby.'

'They would,' said Pink-Whistle, earnestly.
'I've watched them with their dolls for a long
time, and I tell you they could do everything
just as well as you could. Anyway, you're here
to tell them exactly what to do!'

The baby began to wail. Rose ran to it and
picked it up gently. She held it against her
shoulder, and patted it and talked to it. It
stopped crying at once.

'There!' said Pink-Whistle, pleased. 'What
did I tell you? I'll go now and come back in
an hour's time to take the twins home.'

Well, those twins had a most wonderful
time. 'Isn't the baby warm and soft and

57

cuddly?' said Rose to Daisy. 'Look at his downy curls – and see his tiny nails!'

'He's holding on to my finger,' said Daisy. 'Do you want your bath, Baby? I'll get it ready.'

Mrs Jones, the young mother, told the twins where everything was. Before long the baby was in his bath, crowing and splashing. Then he was out on Daisy's lap, being patted dry. Then he was powdered by Rose, who also brushed his soft curls.

'I'll clear away the bath water and hot up his bottle, while you hold him,' she said to Daisy. 'Then it will be my turn to hold him, and I'll give him his bottle.'

Mrs Jones watched the twins in surprise and delight. Why, these children loved her baby and looked after him as well as she did. What loving little hearts they must have – and how clever of that funny little man to find them for her!

Soon the baby was having his bottle on Rose's knee, happy and warm and cuddlesome. Rose looked down on him and thought what a wonderful thing it was to have something warm and living to hold instead of her cold, rather hard dolls – though she did love them, of course. But a baby was so different!

Daisy helped Mrs Jones to get to bed. Then she brought her a boiled egg and some bread and butter, and made her some cocoa. 'You good, kind children!' said Mrs Jones. 'I simply don't know what I should have done without you.'

The twins laid the baby in his cot. He was almost asleep. He hung on to Rose's finger as if he would never let it go. He made a little cooing noise.

'Listen – he's saying thank you!' said Rose.

There came a soft knock at the front door.

'That's Mr Pink-Whistle come to fetch us home,' said Daisy. She went to open the door and Mr Pink-Whistle walked in, beaming all over his face, to see Mrs Jones tucked up in bed, drinking cocoa, and the baby fast asleep in his cot.

'Well – had a good time, everybody?' he asked.

'Lovely!' said the twins. 'Dear Mr Pink-Whistle, thank you for thinking of us.'

'I'm much better now,' said young Mrs Jones. 'I shall be quite all right in the morning, and able to look after Baby myself.'

'Oh, will you?' said the twins, in such disappointed tones that Mr Pink-Whistle laughed.

'Surely you're not sorry that Mrs Jones is better?' he said.

'Well – we're glad about that – but sorry she'll be able to look after the baby herself,' said Rose.

'We do so love him,' said Daisy. 'We've always wanted a real live baby, Mr Pink-Whistle. And we've only had a taste of this once, you see.'

'And it's Saturday tomorrow, and we could have looked after him all day long,' said Rose.

'Especially as our mother is going out for the day and we'll be alone except for Janet our home-help.'

'Look here, dears, if you're going to be alone you come and spend the day with me,' said Mrs Jones. 'I'll give you a lovely lunch and make you a treacle pudding – and we'll have a chocolate cake for tea, and banana sandwiches. And you shall take Baby out in his pram.'

'Do you mean it?' said Rose, her eyes shining. 'Take him out in his pram! Oh, we should feel grand after wheeling our tiny dolls' prams! We'd love to come, Mrs Jones.'

'Would you come to tea, too, Mr Pink-Whistle?' asked Mrs Jones.

'I'd love to,' said Pink-Whistle, beaming. 'My word – two nice children and a baby to play with. I'll be very, very lucky!'

Well, the twins went for the day and Mr Pink-Whistle went to tea, and I couldn't really tell you who was the happiest in that little house – Mrs Jones, or Mr Pink-Whistle, or the twins, or the baby.

And now the twins go to Mrs Jones every single day after school to play with a real live baby instead of dolls – though they haven't forgotten their dolls, of course. They have a wonderful time with the baby – but just wait till they see his very first tooth. It's coming through tomorrow, and nobody knows yet – except Mr Pink-Whistle.

He knows so much, doesn't he? It must be nice to put so many things right. I hope he'll be along the day things go wrong with you!

Chapter 5

Mr Pink-Whistle and the Balloon

There was once a little girl who loved balloons very much indeed. Her name was Susie, and whenever she went to a party, which was about once a year, she always hoped that she would be given a balloon, and sometimes she got her wish.

Now Susie very badly wanted a blue balloon. She had had a red one, and a yellow one, and a green one – but she had never had a blue one.

'I think blue balloons are the prettiest of all,' said Susie. 'I wish I could have a blue balloon on a long piece of string. I'd show it to all the other children.'

Now one day a balloon-seller came to Susie's village. She carried behind her a great bunch of balloons to sell to the children. They were the biggest and most beautiful that the boys and girls had ever seen.

Susie ran to look at them. The balloon-seller had a little stool with her, and she sat down on this at a corner. 'Buy a balloon!' she kept shouting. 'Buy a balloon!'

'How much are they?' asked Susie, 'I've fifty pence at home.'

'What, fifty pence for beautiful big balloons like these!' cried the balloon-seller. 'No, no – these are one pound fifty each, and well worth it, too.'

'Oh – one pound fifty!' said Susie, disappointed. 'That's very dear. But oh, look at that lovely blue one there! How I would like to have it!'

She stared at the blue balloon. It really was the biggest of the bunch, and it bobbed up and down as the breeze took it. Susie felt that she simply must have it.

'I must earn some money!' she thought. 'If only I could get another pound. Then with my fifty pence I should have one pound fifty, and that would be enough.'

64

She walked down the road, thinking hard.

She passed Mrs Jones in her garden, and Mrs Jones called out to her.

'Susie! Whatever are you thinking about? You do look so solemn!'

'I'm thinking how I can earn a pound,' said Susie. 'It's very difficult. I do so want to buy a blue balloon.'

'Well, now I want a little job doing,' said Mrs Jones, 'and I'm willing to give fifty pence for it. I want a parcel taken down to the post office.'

'Oh, I can do that for you,' said Susie.

'It's a heavy parcel, and the post office is a long way off,' said Mrs Jones. 'You'd better see the parcel before you decide. I wanted my Jack to take it for me, but he's had to go to bed with a bad cold, and I can't leave him and take it myself.'.

Mrs Jones showed Susie the parcel. It certainly was rather large. 'But I can carry it all right,' said Susie, 'and I do so badly want the balloon that I'd be glad to take an even heavier parcel for you!'

The little girl set off to the post office. The parcel certainly was heavy! It made her arms ache before she had gone very far. In fact, by the time she had almost reached the post office, she had to stop and rest. She put the parcel down on a little wall, and hung her tired arms down.

And it was there that our old friend, kind Mr Pink-Whistle, met her. He was coming up the street, looking about him as usual, when he saw Susie.

'Hello, little girl!' he said. 'That seems a very heavy parcel to carry!'

'Well, it is rather,' said Susie. 'My arms ache a lot. But I'm having a rest now.'

'Let me carry it the rest of the way for you,' said Mr Pink-Whistle.

'No, thank you,' said Susie. 'You see, I am

earning fifty pence for taking it to the post office, and if you carried it for me, it wouldn't be quite fair to get the fifty pence.'

'I see,' said Mr Pink-Whistle. 'I am very pleased to meet a child who knows what is fair and what is not. Do you want fifty pence for anything special?'

'I do, rather,' said Susie. 'Have you seen the balloon-seller at the corner? Well, she has a most beautiful big blue balloon, and I am longing to buy it. I have never in my life had a blue balloon, you know. It costs one pound fifty, and I am earning fifty pence towards it. I have fifty pence already, and when I earn another fifty pence then I can buy the blue balloon.'

The little girl picked up the parcel and went on again, smiling at Mr Pink-Whistle. He went on his way, too, hoping that Susie would be able to buy what she wanted.

Susie was tired when she got back to Mrs Jones. She was pleased to have a nice bright fifty pence. She put it into her pocket and ran home.

She told her mother about the fifty pence, and how much she wanted to earn another fifty pence to buy the balloon.

'Well, Susie dear,' said her mother, 'If you want to earn fifty pence, you can turn out the hall cupboard, and make it tidy for me.'

Susie didn't like turning out cupboards, because spiders sometimes lived in cupboards, and she was afraid of them. Still, it would be lovely to earn the last fifty pence towards the blue balloon!

So off she went to the hall cupboard with a duster, a dustpan, and a brush. She emptied out all the boots and shoes, bats and balls, and the things that usually live in hall cupboards, and then she swept the cupboard

out well, and dusted it round. She put back all the things very neatly and tidily, felt glad there had been no spider, and called to her mother to come and see if she had done her job properly.

'That's very nice, Susie,' said Mother. 'Here is your fifty pence. Now you can go and buy your blue balloon!'

Susie was excited. She took the pound she had and the fifty pence Mrs Jones had given her, and off she went to the balloon-seller. The big blue balloon was still there, floating at the top of the bunch! Lovely!

Susie gave the woman her one pound fifty, and went off with the glorious blue balloon. It really was very big indeed, and was exactly the colour of the sky in April, so you can guess what a pretty blue it was.

And just as she got round the corner, who should come along but Big Jim! Big Jim was a horrid boy, who loved to tease all the little children. Susie was afraid of him, because Big Jim often pulled her hair and pinched her.

She turned back, but Big Jim had seen her. He came running after her.

'Let's have a look at your balloon!' he shouted. 'Let me hold the string.'

Now Susie knew quite well that if she let Big Jim hold the string, he would go off with her lovely balloon and she would never see it again. So she held it very tightly, and shook her curly head.

'If you don't let me hold your balloon I'll burst it!!' said Big Jim. 'Look – see this pin? Well, I'll stick it right into your balloon if you won't let me hold it!'

Susie held the string fast and began to run down the road. Big Jim ran after her and caught her. He made a jab at the balloon with the pin.

POP!

The balloon burst! Susie stared in horror. Instead of a marvellous blue balloon bobbing in the air there was now only a ragged bit of blue rubber on the ground. Susie burst into loud sobs. How she sobbed.

It is always a dreadful shock to any child when a balloon goes pop, but it was extra dreadful to Susie, because she had worked so hard to get the money for it. Big Jim gave a loud laugh and ran off. He thought he had played a fine joke on Susie.

Susie sobbed and sobbed. She really felt as if her heart was broken. She didn't hear footsteps coming up close to her – but she suddenly felt an arm round her shoulder.

'What's the matter, my dear?' said a kind voice – and, lo and behold, it was Mr Pink-Whistle again! He had heard the sound of crying, and come along to see what was the matter.

'Oh, it's my beautiful blue balloon!' wept Susie. 'Big Jim burst it with a pin because I wouldn't let him hold it. And I worked so hard to get a pound to buy it. And now it's gone. And the balloon-seller hasn't another blue balloon at all. It was the only one.'

'It's a shame!' said Mr Pink-Whistle fiercely. 'It's not fair! I won't have it! Where does Big Jim live?'

'At the first house round the corner,' wept Susie. 'But even if you go and scold him, it won't bring back my balloon, will it?'

'You go home and cheer up,' said Mr Pink-Whistle. 'I'll be along this evening with a surprise. Now, dry your eyes and smile. That's better! goodbye!'

And off went Mr Pink-Whistle to Big Jim's. My, what a surprise was coming to that bad boy!

Mr Pink-Whistle looked very angry as he

marched down the street. He turned the
corner, and came to the first house there.
That was where Big Jim lived. Mr Pink-
Whistle looked over the hedge.

He could hear a boy whistling in one of the
rooms upstairs. That must be Big Jim. Pink-
Whistle muttered a few strange words to
himself – and in a trice he had disappeared!
He was still there, of course, but nobody
could see him except any of the fairy-folk.

Pink-Whistle went round the back way. The
kitchen door was open, and he slipped
inside. A lady was there, doing some washing
up, but she didn't see Pink-Whistle, of course.
He went into the hall and up the stairs,
frightening the cat who had no idea that
anybody was there – and yet she could hear
footsteps!

Big Jim was in his bedroom, putting six big
beautiful glass marbles away in their box. He
was very proud indeed of those marbles.
They were the nicest in the town, and all the
boys at Jim's school loved them and wished
they were theirs. But Jim was not going to give
any away! Not he!

'Are you the bad boy that burst Susie's
balloon?' asked Pink-Whistle in a deep voice

just near to Big Jim's ear. The boy nearly jumped out of his skin.

'Oooooh!' he said in a fright, looking all round. But, of course, he could see no one at all.

'Did you hear what I *said*?' boomed Pink-Whistle. 'I said, "Are you the bad boy that burst Susie's balloon?"'

'I – I – I – did burst a b-b-b-b-balloon,' stammered Big Jim in a fright. 'It was an accident.'

'That's not the *truth*!' said Pink-Whistle angrily. 'You did it on purpose.'

'Who are you?' asked Big Jim. 'And where are you? I can't see anybody. I'm frightened.'

'Good!' said Pink-Whistle. 'Very good. You deserve to be frightened. Now – I'm going to make blue balloons out of something belonging to you! What have you got to give me?'

'Nothing,' said Big Jim. 'I haven't any balloons – or anything in the least like balloons.

'What were those things you were putting into a box?' asked Pink-Whistle, and he opened the lid of the marble-box. Inside lay the greeny-bluey-yellow glass marbles, winking and blinking in their box. 'Ah – marbles! These will do nicely. You shall give me these.'

'Indeed I shan't!' said Big Jim, snatching the box away as it rose into the air, lifted by Pink-Whistle's invisible hand. 'Nobody shall have those. They are my own special best marbles, the finest in the town! Put them down!'

Well, Pink-Whistle was not going to be spoken to like that! He pinched Jim's hand, and the boy gave a yell and dropped the box of marbles. They rolled all over the floor.

'Pick them up and give them to me,' ordered Pink-Whistle. Jim wouldn't. He just stood there, sulking to see his precious marbles scattered over the floor. And then suddenly an invisible hand did to him what he had often done to smaller boys and girls. His hair was pulled!

'Ow!' said Big Jim. 'Don't! Oh, if only I could get hold of you! Wouldn't I pull your hair!'

'Pick up those marbles!' ordered Pink-Whistle again, and his voice was so cold and angry that Big Jim found himself bending down and picking them all up. He put them back into the box.

Pink-Whistle, still invisible, took a piece of chalk from his pocket and drew a little circle on the floor. He put one of the marbles into it.

Then he muttered some words that sounded rather strange and frightening to Jim, and emptied a little blue powder over the big glass marble.

'Now, blow hard on your marble until I tell you to stop,' commanded Pink-Whistle. 'Go on. Kneel down and blow. Quick!'

Big Jim was so afraid of having his hair pulled again that he did as he was told. He knelt down and blew on the marble – and a very strange and peculiar thing happened! It began to blow up, just as a balloon does when breath is blown into it! It changed from a round glass marble with yellow and green streaks in it, to a fine big yellow-green balloon. Marvellous!

'Oooh, that's funny,' said Big Jim. 'My glass marble has changed into a balloon. I shall like taking that about with me.'

'It's not for you,' said Pink-Whistle, taking the balloon out of the circle and quickly tying a piece of string on to it. 'It's for Susie. Now here's the next one. Blue, please!'

Mr Pink-Whistle put a blue-green marble into the circle of chalk and once again Big Jim had to blow. How he blew! He didn't want to, but he was really afraid of the person he couldn't see but could only hear and feel!

That marble blew up into a balloon too – a fine bluey-green one that Pink-Whistle quickly tied up with another piece of string.

Then into the circle went the third marble. 'Oh, I say,' said Big Jim. 'I'm not going to have any more of my beautiful glass marbles changed into balloons. I just won't have it!'

A hard hand came out and caught hold of Jim's right ear, just in the same way that Jim

had so often taken hold of other people's ears! His head was pulled towards the circle, and he had to blow! He blew and he blew. That marble was very hard to blow up, but Pink-Whistle didn't leave go his hold on Jim's ear until the balloon was really quite enormous.

Well, Big Jim had to blow all his precious marbles into balloons! Soon there were six fine balloons waving in the bedroom on the end of strings – and the box of marbles was empty!

'Thank you,' said Pink-Whistle, taking all the strings into one hand, 'Susie shall have all

these. I am sure she will especially love this big blue one made out of your best blue marble, because it is almost exactly the colour of the one you burst. Well, goodbye.'

'Don't take those balloons to Susie,' said Big Jim with tears in his eyes. 'You know quite well they are really my marbles that you've changed by some magic. Please, please, don't take them.'

'How many times have children said, "Please, please," to you, Big Jim, when you have been unkind to them?' asked Pink-Whistle. 'Did you take any notice? No, you didn't. Well, neither shall I. You needed a lesson, my boy, and you've had it. Learn from it and it won't be wasted. You have had to give up something you really loved yourself in order to make up for robbing someone else of something they loved. Remember what it feels like, and be kinder in future!

Off went the little brownie-man, taking the string of balloons with him. He met Jim's mother in the hall, and she was most amazed and astonished to see a string of balloons going through the hall by themselves – for she couldn't see anyone holding them, of course!

'Pardon me, Madam!' said Pink-Whistle politely, forgetting that he was invisible.

'Oh! Gracious me – talking balloons!' cried Jim's mother, and fled into the kitchen. Pink-Whistle chuckled, and went out of the front door. He trotted along to Susie, first making himself seen, because he knew that people would be most astonished to see balloons floating down the street by themselves.

He came to Susie's house. Susie was in the front garden. Her eyes were red, and she looked sad. When she saw Pink-Whistle coming along with a whole bunch of balloons, she gave a squeal of delight.

'Oh! What marvellous balloons! Oh, where did you get that wonderful blue one from? It's even bigger than the one Big Jim burst!'

'I got these from Big Jim,' said Pink-Whistle. 'I made them from his precious marbles! They are stronger than ordinary balloons, my dear. Take them and enjoy them!'

Susie took the strings, going red with surprise and delight. 'Oh!' she said, 'I shall give a tea-party, and let each of my guests have a balloon to take home.'

'Well, the big blue one is especially yours,' said Pink-Whistle. 'Be sure you keep that!'

So Susie did, of course, and she still has it hanging in her bedroom. She gave the others away at a party, and how the children loved them! Wouldn't it be nice if Pink-Whistle came along when any of our balloons went POP? Well – you never know!

Chapter 6

Mr Pink-Whistle Is Rather Funny

O nce when Mr Pink-Whistle was walking down a rather lonely road he met a small boy who was crying bitterly.

Pink-Whistle could never bear to see anyone unhappy, and stopped at once.

'What's the matter?' he said. 'You tell me what's the matter, and maybe I can put it right.'

'My mother s-s-sent me to buy some b-b-bread,' wept the small boy, 'and the boy who lives round the corner took the money from me and ran off with it. And my mother will s-s-s-scold me.'

'Dear, dear!' said Pink-Whistle. 'I'm very

sorry to hear that. Come with me, and we'll buy the bread together. Then maybe if we meet this bad boy you can point him out to me.'

So they went to the baker's shop together and bought some bread. Pink-Whistle paid for it, and they went out in the street again.

But the bad boy was nowhere to be seen. So Pink-Whistle said goodbye and sent the small boy home.

He set off down the road again, a little plump man with the pointed ears of a brownie, and a merry, twinkling look in his eyes. But soon he heard the sound of sobbing again, and he saw two little girls running on the opposite side of the road, tears pouring down their red cheeks.

'Dear, dear me!' said Pink-Whistle to himself. 'All the children seem to be in tears today!'

He ran across and stopped the two little girls. They hadn't any hankies, so he dried their tears with his great big one.

'Now, you tell me what's wrong,' he said.

'Well, we were going to the sweet-shop to buy some chocolate,' said one of the little girls, 'and a horrid boy came up to us and asked us where we were going. And when we told him we were going to the sweet-shop he said how much money had we?'

'And when we showed him, he snatched it out of our hands and ran away,' wept the other little girl. 'So we can't buy our chocolate, and we saved up a whole week for it.'

'Well, well,' said Pink-Whistle, holding out his hand. 'Come along and we'll go and buy some. I don't think that bad boy will stop you if you are with me.'

So they all went to the sweet-shop, and Pink-Whistle bought plenty of chocolate for the two little girls. They beamed at him.

'Oh, thank you! You are kind!' they said. 'We do hope we shan't meet that big boy and have him take our chocolate from us!'

'I'll see you right home,' said Pink-Whistle. So off they went, and he saw them safely home. But they didn't meet the bad boy as Pink-Whistle had hoped they would.

Now, just after he had left them, what should he hear but yet another child crying. Surely it couldn't be someone that bad boy had robbed again? Mr Pink-Whistle hurried round the corner to see.

A very small girl was there, holding the corner of her dress to her eyes. 'He took the sausages!' she wept. 'He dragged them away from me!'

'Who did?' asked Pink-Whistle sharply.

'A bad boy,' wept the tiny girl. 'My mother will scold me for coming home without the sausages. It's that bad boy. He takes everything we have.'

Well, Pink-Whistle had to buy a string of sausages then. It was really quite an expensive morning for him. He didn't see the bad boy. He wondered where he was.

'Nobody really knows,' said the little girl, who was now all smiles again, trotting along by Pink-Whistle, holding tightly to his hand. 'You see, he hides – and pounces out. We never see him come. He runs so fast, too, no one can ever catch him.'

'I see,' said Pink-Whistle. 'Well, I shall look out for him!'

'You'll never see him,' said the tiny girl. 'He only pounces out on children smaller than himself. If you were a child, going shopping, you would see him soon enough!'

Pink-Whistle thought that was a good idea. Of course – he was sure to see that bad boy if he were a small child! It was only small children he robbed.

So, as soon as the small girl had run in at her gate. Pink-Whistle stepped into a lonely passage and muttered a few magic words. And no sooner were the words said than he had gone as small as a child of six!

He looked a bit strange because he still wore his own clothes. But that didn't bother Pink-Whistle. He murmered a few more words and hey presto, he was dressed like a little boy, in shirt and trousers!

Pink-Whistle set out along the street,

carrying a big teddy bear, which had appeared at the same time as the shirt and trousers. He met one or two grown-ups who didn't take any notice of him at all.

He turned down another road where there was not a soul to be seen. He had gone about half-way when he came to an empty house and garden – and out of the gate darted a big boy, about fourteen, with a horrid, spiteful face.

'Stop,' said the big boy, and Pink-Whistle stopped. 'Give me that bear!' said the boy.

'No,' said Pink-Whistle. But the boy snatched the bear roughly from his hands and ran off with it.

He didn't run far, because something very peculiar happened. The bear bit him!

The bad boy felt the nip in his hand and looked down in astonishment. He thought something had stung him. The bear bit him again, and the boy cried out in alarm. He tried to drop the teddy bear, but the bear hung on to him for all it was worth, biting and nipping whenever it could find a bit of flesh.

'Ooooh!' said the boy in great alarm. 'Are you alive? Stop it! That hurt!'

But the bear climbed all over him, biting and snapping, having a perfectly lovely time. Then it slipped down the boy's leg and ran all the way back to Pink-Whistle. The little man whispered to it and it disappeared into thin air. So did Pink-Whistle

He followed the bad boy, then slipped ahead of him, made himself visible and turned back to meet him again. There was no one else about at all.

As Pink-Whistle, who had now changed himself into a little girl, came near the bad boy, he jingled some money in his hand. The bad boy stopped at once.

'Give me that money!'

'No,' said Pink-Whistle, and pretended to cry in fright. The bad boy caught hold of his hand, forced it open roughly and took out the coins Pink-Whistle was holding. He ran off with them.

Pink-Whistle stood and watched. Presently the bad boy stopped and looked down at the money in his hand. The coins seemed to be awfully hot!

'Funny!' said the boy. 'They are almost burning my hand, they're so hot! Ow! I'll put them into my pockets!'

So he did – but they got hotter and hotter and hotter, and the boy could feel them burning a hole and hurting him! Then, to his horror, he saw smoke coming from his pockets! He turned them inside out and the pennies rolled away. But oh, what holes they had burnt!

The bad boy went on, puzzled. He didn't hear Pink-Whistle coming past him, invisible, his feet making no noise at all.

And when he met the little man again, he did not look like Mr Pink-Whistle, but like a sturdy little boy, carrying a small bag in which were some fine glass marbles.

The bad boy stopped and looked at the bag. 'What's in there?' he said roughly.

'My marbles,' said Pink-Whistle in a little-boy voice.

'Let me see them,' said the bad boy.

'No,' said Pink-Whistle.

'You let me see them!' roared the bad boy, and Pink-Whistle meekly opened the bag. In a trice the big boy snatched it away, marbles and all, for he could see what fine ones they were.

Then off he ran. Pink-Whistle stood and watched him.

The bag felt very heavy after a bit. The boy looked down at it. It seemed bigger than he thought – almost a little sack. He decided to put it over his shoulder. It would be easier to carry that way.

So he put it over his left shoulder and set off again. But with every step he took the sack felt heavier and heavier and heavier. It weighed the boy down. He tried to take it off his shoulder, but he couldn't. He panted and puffed, and at last stopped, almost squashed to bits under the enormous weight.

Some children came running by and they stopped in surprise to see the bad boy weighed down by the enormous sack. They all knew him. He had taken things from each one of them at some time or other.

'What a horrid smell the sack has!' said one child. 'What's in it?'

'Help me to get it off my shoulder!' begged the bad boy. One of the children slit a hole in the sack – and out came a stream of rotten apples!

'Ho! He's carrying rotten apples!' cried the child. 'Where did you steal those?'

'They're marbles, not apples!' said the bad boy, in surprise. But they weren't. He was carrying nothing but hundreds of rotten apples! How extraordinary.

And then the children had a lovely time. They pulled the sack away from the bad boy, spilt all the rotten apples, and pelted him with them as hard as they could. Pink-Whistle joined in, you may be sure. A good punishment was just what the bad boy needed!

He ran off at last, crying bitterly, for he was not at all brave. Pink-Whistle, now looking like a little girl, met him as he went down the road. Pink-Whistle carried a hand-bag, and felt certain that the boy would stop.

But he didn't. He had had enough of taking things away from children. There was something peculiar about that day. So Pink-Whistle, looking just like a nice little girl, stopped the boy instead.

'I've got a whole pound in my bag!' said Pink-Whistle, shaking it so that the money jingled.

'Keep it!' said the bad boy, wiping his dirty, tear-stained face.

'There's nobody about. You can easily take it away from me!' said Pink-Whistle.

'I'm never going to take anything from anyone again,' said the boy. 'Never!'

Pink-Whistle suddenly changed into himself again, and to the boy's enormous surprise the little girl was no longer there – but a solemn-faced little man stood in front of him.

'Do you mean that?' asked Pink-Whistle, sternly. 'Or do you want a few more lessons?'

'Oh, no, no!' cried the boy. 'I'd be afraid of stopping anyone now. You've no idea the awful things that have happened to me today!'

'Serves you right,' said Pink-Whistle. 'Now you listen to me. You be kind in future to all those children you've stolen from, and give them money and sweets whenever you can. That will show me you're sorry. See? Else maybe awful things will happen to you again!'

'I will, I will,' promised the bad boy, and ran home, frightened and worried. He thought about it the whole afternoon, and decided that he had better keep his word.

So, to the great astonishment of all the small children round about, the bad boy stopped them and gave them things, instead of taking things away from them. And soon they were very fond of him, and ran to meet him whenever they saw him.

'I wish I could meet that funny little fellow again and tell him how much happier I am now,' the bad boy thought to himself a great many times. 'He might like me. I wish I could meet him.'

But Pink-Whistle was far away by that time, putting something else right. I do hope he comes along if anything goes wrong for you!